This Little Tiger book
belongs to:

_____

_____

_____

For Joey and Ciara ~ two little ones
who are a big part of my world ~ DVB

For little Levi Louis ~ T W

LITTLE TIGER PRESS
An imprint of Magi Publications
1 The Coda Centre, 189 Munster Road, London SW6 6AW
www.littletigerpress.com

First published in Great Britain 2008
This edition published 2010

Text copyright © Magi Publications 2008
Illustrations copyright © Tim Warnes 2008
Tim Warnes has asserted his right to be identified as the illustrator
of this work under the Copyright, Designs and Patents Act, 1988

A CIP catalogue record for this book is available from the British Library

All rights reserved • ISBN 978-1-84506-648-2

Printed in Belgium

LTP/1300/0070/0210 • 10 9 8 7 6 5 4 3

I Love You as BIG as the World

David Van Buren

Tim Warnes

LITTLE TIGER PRESS
London

I love you as
big as the
world.

I love you as deep as the sea.

I love you as
bright
as the sun.

I love you.

And **I know** you love me!

I love you

as blue as the sky.

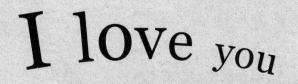

I love you as long as the days.

I love you as

high as the mountain top.

I love you in so many ways!

I love you
as strong

as the wind.

I love you as soft as the dew.

I love you as far as a star.

I love you because . . .

. . . you are

you!